# DADDY'S PETTING ZOO

Illustrations by Kenny Estrella

Sheri Haynes

To order additional copies of this book, contact:
Xlibris Corporation
1-888-795-4274
www.Xlibris.com
Orders@Xlibris.com

# Dedication

This book is dedicated to my precious father, Ira Haynes, together we shared such a love for animals. Ira lived to be the oldest businessman in Manhattan, Kansas.He owned a barbershop for over 61 years across the street from Kansas State University. This business is now owned by my brother, Ira Haynes Jr.The Haynes Style Shop has been in our family for over 95 years. My mother LaDonna Haynes, who was so supportive and such a wonderful mother. She helped care for all of the animals and especially loved the swans.I want to thank my brother for putting up with me and the horses I sent to him.This is also dedicated to my grandchildren, Chad, Justin, Chris, and Tommy.What a blessing to have such a wonderful family!

Once on a lovely ranch lived two swans named Hansel & Gretel. They had two big ponds and lived with two other black swans named Romeo & Juliet. There were two big black Rottweiler's, Duke and Raja plus cats, ducks, chickens, peacocks, horses. The girl Cher & her dad loved all of the animals very much. Hansel and the girl were very close. Often times Cher would put a blanket down on the grass under a big shade tree to read a story and Hansel would lay down beside her.

Cher's father was very old and he loved to sit in the big green grassy yard by the

pond and watch all of the animals with his daughter. This was their special place and

Cher and her father would sit together for hours with a fire in the fire pit burning

slowly and just watch all the funny things the animals would do. The father was 87

Years old so this was a very special time they spent together.

Mork and Mendy were two little goats. They would come running to Cher in the morning. Mork could easily jump over the little pond on the way to the gate to meet her. Mendy just couldn't seem to make it over the pond so she sometimes ended up in the pond, with a big splash! She always tried to jump over it anyway. Hansel the big white swan did rule the yard. Even the big dogs stayed out of his way. I think they were a bit afraid of him. He was the boss of the yard and if those dogs got in his way he would spread his big wings and chase them. Hansel was in total control of that petting zoo and all of the animals respected him. The dogs protected all of the animals from predators that would come near the yard. Raja liked to pick up a chicken and carry it around the yard. We would say "Drop it" and the chicken would just fly off. They were all a big happy family.

Mork & Mendy would play King of the Mountain and jump on top of this big rock, butt heads and knock each other off of the rock. They thought this was great fun. Well one day Mr. Fluff, who was a Chinese silky chicken jumped on the rock as they were playing. The goats accidentally knocked him off the rock. Well he flew up in the air and landed in a big bucket of water. He always thought he was the head rooster of the petting zoo so this was quite embarrassing for him.

Daddy's four year old grandson, Chad, had his own miniature Shetland pony

named Peanuts. She would run around the yard with him, then stop and he

would brush her and play with her. All the animals in the petting zoo loved Chad.

His grandfather loved watching Chad play with all of the animals,

Daddy and Hansel would tease each other. Hansel would try and sneak up on the father and give him a little peck. Or, if Daddy would sit in the gazebo near the pond Hansel would see him, jump in the pond, and splash him with his big wings. It was so funny to watch them. Hansel really thought he was such a big Boy.

One day Cher found out that she had to leave the big beautiful home and find homes for all of their precious animals they both loved so much. So one by one she found families that would love the animals and take good care of them. It wasn't that easy to find a home with ponds big enough for four swans. Cher's mother had bought a home in the desert with four big ponds that would be just perfect for these swans. Cher's mom loved these swans and was determined to make a lovely home for them. So this would be just perfect. White swans could be in the ponds on the west side of this huge retirement development. The black swans on the east side. This way there would be no fighting for their territory. Now they could choose a beautiful pond to raise their babies on.

Cher and her mom were very pleased and everyone the park just fell in love with Hansel and Gretel. People just loved to stroll by the lake and watch the swans.

By now Hansel and Gretel were 3 years old. That's how old swans have to be to mate and have babies. So Hansel got busy making nests for Gretel. She was so picky and Hansel worked so hard. Hansel worked days and swan's nests have to be really big. Well Gretel didn't like the first one and messed it up. So Hansel set out to make a second nest. Gretel didn't like that one either. She even messed that one up and just walked off with her beak in the air. So Hansel thought, I know, I will make the best nest ever and he found some tall Pampas grass. Now this grass stands up and is at least 4 ft tall. Somehow he got to the top of the grass and made Gretel a nest that looked out over the lake. He even built a slide into the water so Gretel could take a break from the summer heat. She loved it! Hansel was so proud!

Now Gretel proceeded to lay her eggs. Hansel would sit down at the bottom of this nest protecting their eggs. They took turns, Gretel sat on the eggs for two hours, and then she would slide into the lake for her break. Hansel immediately took over sitting on the eggs for another two hours. They took turns until the babies hatched.

Everything was fine until the eggs started to hatch. Gretel would slide the new baby down to the water. Dad was waiting to teach them how to swim. It was so amazing! Hansel was so proud! He would put the baby on his back and swim around just to show off. The people around the lake were buzzing with excitement. Then, some weekend camper came in and started teasing Hansel. These were Hansel's babies and it was his job to protect them. Hansel started spreading his wings and chasing everyone away from his lake. Even nice people were coming in their golf carts to see these adorable babies... The resort owners didn't like Hansel chasing people away. So they called Cher's Mom and told her they had to find Hansel and Gretel a new home.

Fortunately Cher's mom had become friends with the lady that takes care of the swans, parrots and flamingo's at a big hotel in Palm Springs. This hotel is surrounded by lakes and just beautiful. Mom called and they were more than happy to take Hansel, Gretel and their babies.

Now the problem of catching all of them and transporting them to the hotel. Several friends offered to help and about 3 hours later they had them safely caged and ready to transport. When driving into the hotel there are lakes, flowers, flamingo's wading in the water and Cher knew this was paradise for Hansel and Gretel.

They decided to let Hansel go into the lake first so he could check it out for Gretel and the babies. But there was another male swan on this lake and he was having no part of Hansel moving into his lake. Now he is chasing Hansel out of the water and Hansel is running across the golf course right through about 10 golfers hitting golf balls. Cher is running right behind Hansel calling all of the golfers to help. They laughed at the sight and pitched right in. Now they are all running after Hansel finally guiding him right into Cher's arms. She held him and loved him and made him feel better. Cher took him to another side of the lake where there were no swans. She let him go, Hansel swam for awhile then came back and gurgled at her.. This was his sign to Cher that it is ok.

Now it was safe for Gretel and the babies, they were released into the water to be with their daddy. Our family stayed and watched them for hours; they settled right in and Hansel swam over to Cher as if to say, thank you. Hansel loved to swim to Cher and show off so she knew he approved. Finally, Cher had found Hansel and his family the most beautiful place in the world to live in and raise Hansel and Gretel's precious baby swans.

CPSIA information can be obtained
at www.ICGtesting.com
Printed in the USA
LVHW07n0220100918
589660LV00004B/22/P